RETURN TO THE
LIBRARY OF DOOM

The Vampire Chapter

BY MICHAEL DAHL

Illustrated by
Bradford Kendall

STONE ARCH BOOKS
a capstone imprint

ZONE BOOKS ARE PUBLISHED BY
STONE ARCH BOOKS
A CAPSTONE IMPRINT
151 GOOD COUNSEL DRIVE, P.O. BOX 669
MANKATO, MINNESOTA 56002
WWW.CAPSTONEPUB.COM

LIBRARY OF CONGRESS CATALOGING-IN-PUBLICATION DATA
DAHL, MICHAEL.
  THE VAMPIRE CHAPTER / WRITTEN BY MICHAEL DAHL ;
ILLUSTRATED BY BRADFORD KENDALL.
       P. CM. -- (RETURN TO THE LIBRARY OF DOOM)
  ISBN 978-1-4342-2143-8 (LIBRARY BINDING)
  (1. VAMPIRES--FICTION. 2. BOOKS AND READING--FICTION. 3.
HORROR STORIES.) I. KENDALL, BRADFORD, ILL. II. TITLE.
  PZ7.D15134VAM 2010
  (FIC)--DC22   2010004058

ART DIRECTOR: KAY FRASER
GRAPHIC DESIGNER: HILARY WACHOLZ
PRODUCTION SPECIALIST: MICHELLE BIEDSCHEID

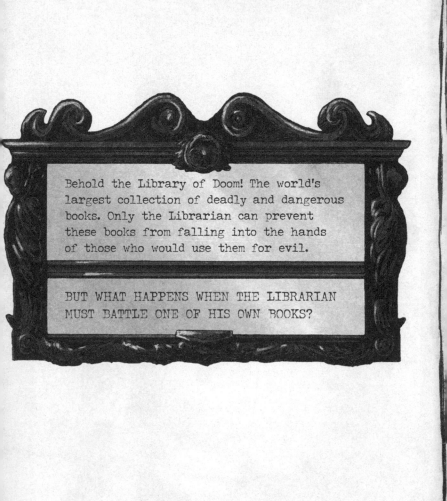

Behold the Library of Doom! The world's
largest collection of deadly and dangerous
books. Only the Librarian can prevent
these books from falling into the hands
of those who would use them for evil.

BUT WHAT HAPPENS WHEN THE LIBRARIAN
MUST BATTLE ONE OF HIS OWN BOOKS?

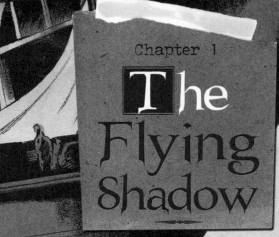

Chapter 1
The Flying Shadow

Harry walks up the **DARK** stairs to his bedroom.

A **shiver** passes through him when he opens the door.

Wind blows the curtains at his window.

On the floor, a book flutters its pages in the COLD breeze.

That's strange, thinks Harry. *I thought I closed that.*

He walks over to the WINDOW.

Suddenly, a shadow rushes past him.

The boy jumps back.

The shadow **FLEW** through his
open window.

It was too LARGE to be a bird.

Harry looks up and sees the same shadow passing in front of the moon.

The shape has long, pointed wings.

They remind him of a **bat**.

The boy shivers again.

He quickly **SHUTS** the window.

He remembers how the shape looked as it flew past him.

He remembers seeing a man's face. The face had sharp, white **TEETH**.

Chapter 2

Holes

Harry picks up a book off the floor. It was the book he was planning to read before bed that night.

His **fingers** feel something <u>odd</u> on the book's cover.

He turns on the **LIGHT** to get a
better look.

"I don't understand," Harry says.

On the cover are two **deep** holes.

Quickly, he **OPENS** the book.

He stares at the pages.

He **turns** the pages faster and faster.

His eyes GROW wide with fear.

He stands up and throws the book away from him.

The book HITS the floor with a loud bang and falls open.

His father **YELLS** from downstairs.

"Harry!" he says. "What's going on? What's that noise?"

"It's nothing," calls Harry. "I just **dropped** my book."

HARRY stares down at the book on the floor.

He can't believe what he sees.

The book is **blank**.

All the words have disappeared.

It looks as if the book has been drained of **INK**.

Chapter 3

The Vampire Book

The next afternoon, Harry meets his friend Jon at the **library**.

"You **BELIEVE** me, don't you?"
Harry asks his friend. "You believe
what I told you about last night?"

"I don't know," says Jon. "Are you
sure you weren't **dreaming?**"

Harry pulls the **EMPTY** book out of his backpack.

He hands it to Jon.

"Look at those holes," Harry says. "What do they remind you of?"

Jon **gently** touches the two holes with his finger.

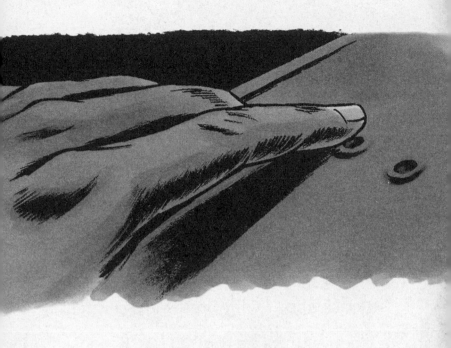

Then he stares up at Harry.

"Vampires," he says.

Harry nods.

"That's why we're here," he
explains. "I know the library has
books about vampires. Maybe it tells
about vampires that **attack** books."

Harry **GLANCES** around the old building.

He searches the **DIM** rooms for his favorite librarian, Mrs. Rook.

Finally, he asks one of the workers where she is.

"Mrs. Rook has been out sick," says the worker. "But you can talk to the **NEW** librarian. His name is Mr. Turner. Mr. Turner mostly works just at night," says the worker. "But I'll see if I can find him."

"That's all right," says Harry. "We'll look for ourselves."

The boys find the section with books about vampires.

The books are in a **DARK**, dusty corner of the library.

They pull several books off the shelves and **flip** through them.

"This book is empty!" cries Jon.

"Just like yours."

All the books that Harry looks
through are also BLANK.

Then Harry sees an old book at
the back of the shelf. It was **hidden**
behind the others.

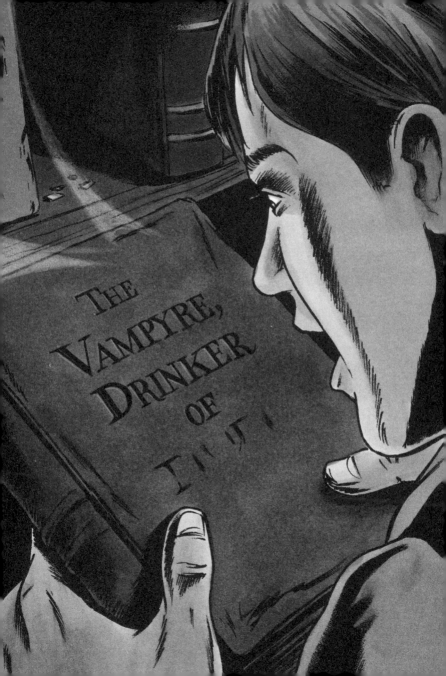

Chapter 4

Disappearing Ink

"This is it!" cries Harry.

They open the book to the table of contents.

"Look," says Jon. "Chapter 37. About Vampires and Books."

They carefully turn the yellow pages to find the chapter.

The boys stare at each other. "It's gone!" Harry says.

The chapter is **missing**.

The pages of the 37th chapter have been **TORN** from the book.

"Now what should we do?" asks Jon.

Harry **STARES** down at the floor, wondering what to do next.

He looks at the floor next to his
shoe. He sees a round, black **dot**. ·

Harry kneels down and looks more
carefully at the dot. "Ink," he says
quietly.

"There's another one," says Jon, pointing.

A second black dot **lies** a few feet away.

The boys see a trail of black dots leading between the shelves.

Without saying a word, both boys follow the **INK**.

Behind them, a gloved hand picks up the vampire book. The ancient book seems to **VIBRATE**.

The cover grows dim and blurry.

Suddenly, the book disappears.

Chapter 5

Family Grave

The boys head out of the building, following the trail of ink drops.

They race down the **stone** steps of the library.

"There are more drops over there," says Jon, pointing.

Behind them, a dark shadow lurks in the library **DOORWAY**.

The inky trail leads through a nearby forest.

Soon, the forest opens up into a
small **CLEARING**.

Moonlight **GLEAMS** on white
stones that poke through the grass.

"It's a graveyard," says Harry.

The boys suddenly freeze.

They hear a **LOUD** creaking sound.
It comes from a stone building on the
other side of the graveyard.

It is a vault, where members of one family are **ENTOMBED** together.

A name is carved into the stone above the vault's doors.

TURNER

The metal doors of the vault are wide open.

Chapter 6
Inside the Coffin

Harry and Jon walk through the metal doors. Their footsteps echo off the stone walls.

Harry sees **flames** up ahead.

As they walk closer, they find hundreds
of burning candles. In the center of the
candles lies a wooden coffin.

"The **vampire**!" whispers Jon.

"It's still daylight out," says Harry. "Everyone knows that vampires can't attack until night."

The boys **STAND** still. They stare at the coffin.

"I think we should leave," says Jon.

Then the wooden coffin **creaks**. Its
heavy lid begins to rise.

A withered, yellow hand slides out
of the coffin.

It pushes the lid all the way **open**.

A dark figure stands up. It TOWERS over the frightened boys.

The figure has long, white teeth. He smacks his pale lips together.

Then he raises a hand and POINTS at Harry.

"Come forward," says the vampire.

Another figure steps out from the
SHADOWS.

The man is the Librarian, the
guardian of the Library of Doom.

"Return to your coffin," he
commands the vampire.

"Never again!" screams the
monster.

Suddenly, a second stranger enters the candlelit room.

"Don't worry," she says to the Librarian. "He won't escape this time."

The man and woman raise their hands.

A silver SCISSORS forms in the air.

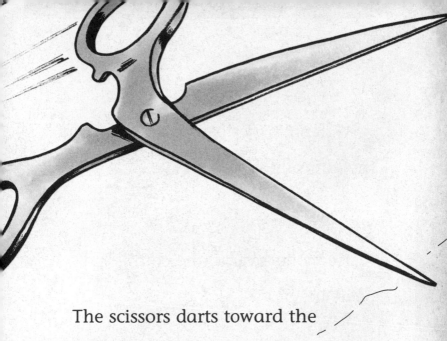

The scissors darts toward the vampire. The evil creature closes his eyes and **SCREAMS**.

"Scissors defeats paper," says the Librarian quietly.

When Harry opens his eyes again, the vampire is **GONE**.

He walks over to the coffin and peers inside.

On the cushions are a few pieces of **OLD** yellow paper.

"It's Chapter 37," he says.

"**Words** are the most powerful weapons in the world," says the Librarian. "That is why he drank the ink from books."

"His name is <u>Draco Papyrus</u>. I followed him to your library," the Librarian explains. "He had stolen and hidden the VAMPYRE book that belonged to me. I brought it back to the Library of Doom before I came here."

The vault begins to **tremble**.

Dust and stones fall from the ceiling. Candles **CRASH** onto the floor.

"Out!" shouts the Librarian. "Now!"

Harry and Jon **RUN** back toward the entrance.

They race through the METAL
doors.

They tumble down the stairs.

Behind them, the stone vault
crumbles into dust.

As they sit on the grass, Harry
REACHES into his backpack.

He pulls out his book.

The two holes are missing. And all
of the words have RETURNED.

Author

Michael Dahl is the author of more than 200 books for children and young adults. He has won the AEP Distinguished Achievement Award three times for his nonfiction. His Finnegan Zwake mystery series was shortlisted twice by the Anthony and Agatha awards. He has also written the Library of Doom series. He is a featured speaker at conferences around the country on graphic novels and high-interest books for boys.

Illustrator

Bradford Kendall has enjoyed drawing for as long as he can remember. As a boy, he loved to read comic books and watch old monster movies. He graduated from Rhode Island School of Design with a BFA in Illustration. He has owned his own commercial art business since 1983, and lives in Providence, Rhode Island, with his wife, Leigh, and their two children Lily and Stephen. They also have a cat named Hansel and a dog named Gretel.

Glossary

ancient (AYN-shunt)—very old

commands (kuh-MANDZ)—orders to do something

dim (DIM)—dark, hard to see

drained (DRAYND)—removed the liquid

echo (EK-oh)—a sound repeating because its sound waves are bouncing off a large surface

entombed (en-TOOMD)—placed in a vault or tomb

guardian (GAR-dee-uhn)—someone who protects something

lurks (LURKS)—tries to hide, for an evil reason

odd (OD)—strange

section (SEK-shuhn)—a part of an area

vault (VAWLT)—a burial chamber

vibrate (VYE-brate)—to move back and forth rapidly

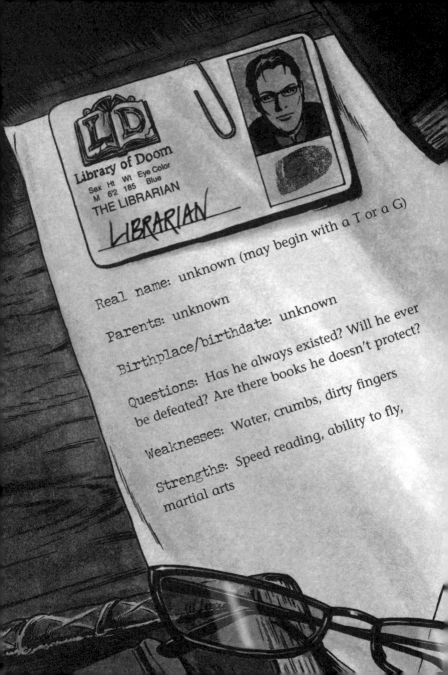

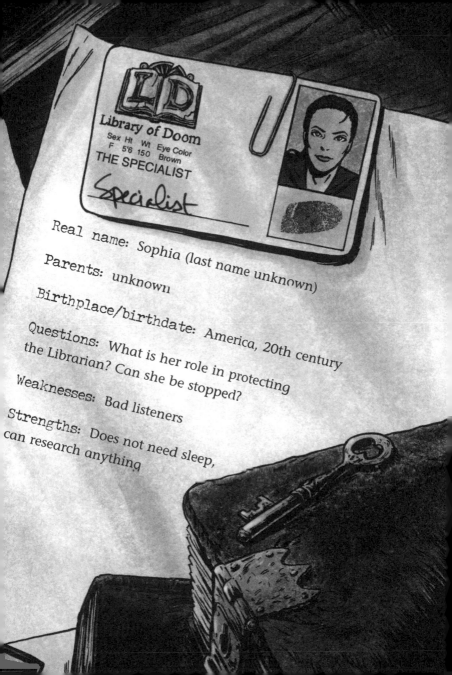

Library of Doom

Sex F Ht 5'6 Wt 150 Eye Color Brown

THE SPECIALIST

Specialist

Real name: Sophia (last name unknown)

Parents: unknown

Birthplace/birthdate: America, 20th century

Questions: What is her role in protecting the Librarian? Can she be stopped?

Weaknesses: Bad listeners

Strengths: Does not need sleep, can research anything

Draco Papyrus was a normal bookseller who lived in England in the 18th Century. But when he was attacked in his bookshop and bitten by a vampire, he too became a bloodsucking beast.

Draco was not an ordinary vampire. He became obsessed with books about vampires. First he was just a collector. He would travel to rare book sales to purchase the books. Soon, he decided that he needed to destroy every book about vampires so that he could protect his kind. When he discovered the Library of Doom, it became his mission to completely destroy it.

The Librarian stopped Draco, but it is rumored that there are more book-destroying vampires still at large.

Discussion Questions

1. How was the vampire **destroying** the books?

2. What did you think about the title of this book? Does it **match** what you felt when you read the story?

3. What were some of the feelings you had when you read this **BOOK?**

Writing Prompts

1. Create your own **VILLAIN**, someone who wants to destroy the Library. What is the villain's name? How can they be stopped?

2. Pretend you're Harry. Write a story for your school newspaper about the things that happened in this book.

3. **CREATE** a cover for a book. It can be this book or another book you like, or a made-up book. Don't forget to write the information on the back, and include the author and illustrator names!